Big Animals
Little Animals

Written by Brylee Gibson

Look at this whale.
This whale is **big**.

Look at the **big** tail.

2

tail

Look at this elephant.
This elephant is **big**.

The legs are **big**.
The ears are **big**, too.

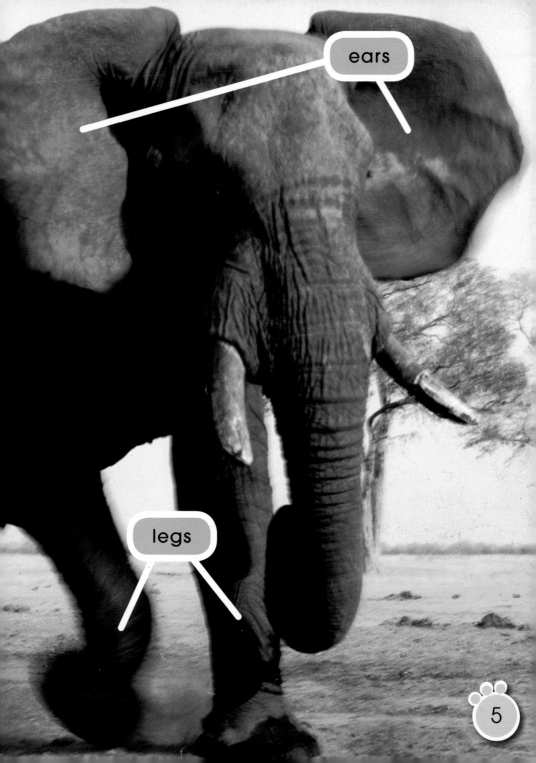

ears

legs

5

mouth

Look at this hippo.
The body is **big**.

The mouth is **big**, too.

body

Look at the ants.
The ants are little.

Look at the little legs.

8

legs

flea

Look at the flea.
The flea is little.

Look at the spider.
The spider is little.

spider

fly

Here is a fly.
Here is a ladybug.

A fly and a ladybug
are little.

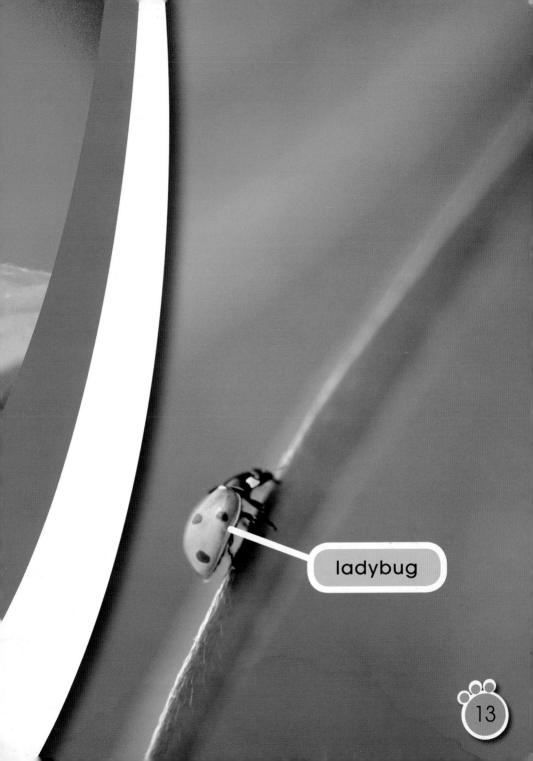

ladybug

gorilla

Here is a gorilla.
Here is a bear.

A gorilla and a bear
are **big**.

14

bear

Index

Guide Notes

> **Title: Big Animals, Little Animals**
> **Stage:** Early (1)— Red
>
> **Genre:** Nonfiction
> **Approach:** Guided Reading
> **Processes:** Thinking Critically, Exploring Language, Processing Information
> **Written and Visual Focus:** Photographs (static images), Index, Labels
> **Word Count:** 102

THINKING CRITICALLY
(sample questions)
- Look at the title and read it to the children.
- Tell the children this book is about big animals and little animals.
- Ask them what some big and little animals are that they know.
- Focus the children's attention on the index. Ask: "What are you going to find out about in this book?"
- If you want to find out about a whale, which page would you look on?
- If you want to find out about a hippo, which page would you look on?
- Look at the whale on page 2 and 3. How do you think the whale's big tail might help it?
- Look at the elephant on page 5. How do you think the elephant's big ears might help it?

EXPLORING LANGUAGE

Terminology
Title, cover, photographs, author, photographer

Vocabulary
Interest words: legs, ears, tail, body
High-frequency words: little, too
Compound word: ladybug

Print Conventions
Capital letter for sentence beginnings, periods, commas